Possession

Also By Angela Ball:

Kneeling Between Parked Cars
Quartet

Possession

Poetry by

Angela Ball

Red Hen Press

1995

Possession

Copyright © 1995 by Angela Ball

All rights reserved. No part of this book may be used or reproduced in any manner whatever without written permission except in the case of brief quotations embodied in critical articles and reviews.

Cover art by Frederick Barthelme

First Edition
ISBN 0-9639528-6-2
Library of Congress Catalog Card Number 95-074670

Red Hen Press
Valentine Publishing Group
Los Angeles, California

ACKNOWLEDGEMENTS

Grateful acknowledgement is made to the editors and publishers of the following anthologies and periodicals, in which the poems in this collection were first published: *The American Voice*: "Lofty Cities." *Field*: "Flash," "The Man in a Shell," "The Nothing Above the Water." *Frank: An International Journal of Contemporary Writing & Art:* "The Kind of Thing That Happens," "Airships." *The Denver Quarterly*: "Embrace," "World-Famous Sex Acts." *The Kenyon Review*: "A Language," "Sky," "Text." *The Literary Review*: "Adjustments." *The Malahat Review*: "The English Artist's Wife," "Elegy for Edgar Allan Poe," "Reflex," "Fiddle Music," "The Dance Pianist," "The Kiss," "The Lady with the Pet Dog." *Northwest Review*: "The Prayer Meeting." *Partisan Review*: "Jamaica." *Ploughshares*: "Hobo," "Captain Cook." *Poetry*: "House," "Body," "Possession." *Prairie Schooner*: "Drive," "No One by That Name," "Counter." *Southern Poetry Review*: "Theater," "Charm." *Stand*: "Towns," "Chassé." *Tel Aviv Review*: "Refugia," "Out of Context," "Night Work," "The Architect." *Virginia Quarterly Review*: "Materials." *Willow Springs*: "Keats in Rome," "A New Exile Talks of His Country."

Table of Contents

ONE

13 : HOBO
15 : HOUSE
16 : POSSESSION
18 : MATERIALS
20 : THE ARCHITECT
22 : JAMAICA
24 : A LANGUAGE
26 : THE KIND OF THING THAT HAPPENS
27 : NIGHT WORK
28 : BODY
30 : LOFTY CITIES

TWO

35 : ELEGY FOR EDGAR ALLAN POE
36 : KEATS IN ROME
38 : CAPTAIN COOK
42 : DESPERATE REMEDY
43 : CHARM

POEMS FOR ANTON CHEKHOV:

47 : FIDDLE MUSIC
48 : THE KISS
50 : THE LADY WITH THE PET DOG
52 : THE DANCE PIANIST
53 : THE MAN IN A SHELL
54 : THEATER

THREE

- 59 : A NEW EXILE TALKS OF HIS COUNTRY
- 60 : REFUGIA
- 62 : ABANDON
- 64 : TOWNS
- 66 : THE FAMILY OF EYES
- 68 : FLASH
- 69 : REFLEX
- 70 : DRIVE
- 72 : THE PRAYER MEETING
- 73 : NO ONE BY THAT NAME
- 75 : COUNTER
- 76 : CHASSÉ
- 77 : ADJUSTMENTS
- 78 : AIRSHIPS
- 80 : OUT OF CONTEXT
- 82 : SKY
- 84 : TEXT
- 86 : WORLD-FAMOUS SEX ACTS
- 88 : TALK
- 89 : EMBRACE
- 90 : THE NOTHING ABOVE THE WATER
- 91 : THE ENGLISH ARTIST'S WIFE

for my mother and father

"We are full of things that impel us outwards." — Blaise Pascal, *Pensées*

One

HOBO

I feel cloudy,
stumble often, knock my skull
on the roof of the car getting in
because I'm having a stint
of daydreams.

In one it's raining, weeks of it,
then for no reason sunlight returns
fingersnapping through trees.

In this one
it's Paris, a lonely attic,
I remove a letter
from its ragged envelope
and read in faded script, "All I want
are your eyes."

These dreams must know
I'll go anywhere.
Mostly I walk around
half here, longing to join a pack of dogs
loping toward adventure.

Here's a reverie about a man who sleeps
with a woman—secretly, in a quarry,
a niche hidden by boulders.
One of her coat buttons
is scraped off
and he holds it an instant in his open palm
before handing it over.

Angela Ball

She's married and sends him away.
He travels his whole life
because there's nothing left
worth stopping for:
only slates of continents,
the shadowy cities with their arteries,
where each great turnpike
fans into the next.

He just wants love's journey
from wonder to fear to ease,
a woman and man arriving at once
from everywhere.

HOUSE

"Whoever has no house now, will never have one." — Max Frisch

Of all building work I like best
the bare structure before the roofs
go on—above it
blue sky, the metallic echo
of blows as they nail down
the boarding. Wood shavings, warm
sawdust, trucks bringing new planks
from the lumberyard. A series of rooms
full of sky—uninterrupted
stories, space seeing sun
for the last time in decades. Morning
sealed before my eyes. My gaze
stills things—the many I know
that are gone. Drugstore with black and white
diamond tiles, black wire chairs with backs
twisted into hearts. Woolworth's
smooth wooden floor. Sanctums.
My home's a meager impression
of bare steps, a kitchen's waxen light
at the end of rain. A closet
with a fifth of whiskey—my parents'
wedding present—glowing intact.
Its darkening amber.

A failed shopping center pales as if to record
a slow cooling of the sun's rays.
What will remain of the flatness
that in time everything takes? Under the town's
thin blanket of lights. "It's inhuman,"
I'm told, "to expect a person to see beyond his own ruin."

Angela Ball

POSSESSION

Anton Chekhov, that good doctor,
says, "Once a man is possessed
by an idea, there's no doing anything with him."

A teacher who cares nothing
for his students keeps his college diploma
in a gilt frame that sets it off
splendidly.

A grandmother has spent her savings
on a famous toy: brightly painted cars
that fly through the air
on wires. Her grandson examines it,
then asks to go and play outside.

A girl, long brilliant
hair, runs fast as she can
through the streets
to her girlfriend's house.
"We made love! He loves me!
And now I know how beautiful
it all is."

A winter night, flames
move inside the grate. He holds her
in his arms; she is thinking
about the price of scallions.

Finally, a man can buy
the jacket he's always prized.
Right away, he notices
a loose thread, knows he'll never find
the courage to pull it.

"How can you laugh at little things?"
a woman asks. "Our baby's
gone, and my life's gone, too."
Soon loss is more precious
than the baby, than anything.

A woman has fallen in love
with a man at her office. He seems
distracted, troubled—it must be
he feels the same. One day he asks
to speak with her in private.
"Excuse me, but this perfume
you're always wearing—it seems
to hurt my sinuses."

The lonely have much in their minds
to talk about.

A wish is all there is,
long payment for something happy.
Every person's guilty
of spring and spring's ending.

Angela Ball

MATERIALS

Parents tell children
you'll get great things
from us someday.
Each time I put away
a crystal vase, several people
hold their breath.

I slip—my sneakers bald,
no purchase left.
A man who was in World War I,
at Paschendaele, tells about mud:
"We couldn't make a forward move
without duck boards, removing them
as we advanced, putting them down again
ahead of us."

An old couple has plenty, but
money is easier to worry
than death. They insure
survival through small observances
of thrift: measure
accurately, remember to consume
perishables.

One day by mistake I drove past
a scrap yard where black men
rearrange smoking wreckage:
raw orange of rusty springs,
angle iron, mud. They wear twisted hats
and the sideways look
of men trapped but resigned.

The place they're buried: sponge patch
of dirt mounds and tumbled plastic flowers.
The epitaphs are someplace else.

Still—many safe investments:
the dust of city sounds,
a midnight parking garage,
an empty bottle in a paper bag
fastened by a twist
to the neck. The dusk
five o'clock takes,
the big highways'
two rainy grooves.
Birds passing high up.

THE ARCHITECT

"The first principle of everything is water." — Thales

The first big building I knew
was the grade school, its entrance
so anxious to be tied to solidity
and grandeur. A building so thick
it was a surprise that the windows
gave onto the outside. Halls
so cool I thought
they were marble.

When I build, the air—
all of it depends on me. Stress
is stress. Every load we omit
in our calculations
must be paid for. Witness
the slides: cracks
above the support, shearing,
torsion in the pillars, collapse.

We had reached the end
of each other. She touched my shirt pocket
lightly, once, sad because loving
but not in love.
I was holding a metal pen
in my right hand.
One sees what one sees. I've given up
thinking about her.

It's the fine moment
before it's cold weather,
light poured of mild lead.
A day lucky enough
to set the wastebasket
right under my throw,
to have a book so new
some of its pages are still
fused. There's mist,
nightfall. My collection
of rock crystals.

Every freak thing
moves toward the normal—witness this
picture of a flood: cattle standing
patiently, mutely on a roof.

JAMAICA

The Mood Club is like the inside
of a hat oranged
with tropical dust, its rows
of rum bottles like the murk
of an old city. Jumpety table
made of old dark wood
for me to sit at and have
a bottle of Red Stripe.
There's something on the wall
behind me—spread thighs
framing my head, a mural of legs
scissored out so far the torso
attached to them seems broken
or sprung. Ashen patch
of dress, the rest
of the figure absent
or totally dark. A man
comes with dominoes, rubs them face down
on the table, and I get mine—
my favorite the one with a single
dot, slow black in all the whiteness.
He shows my thumbs how to command them
all at once to make a fence. Already he's way ahead
of me, eating my plays
alive, clacking down
his last domino—all the time moving
back and forth from the game
to his shaved ice concession
across the street—
he sells most of the color
electric blue. I lay down
more dominoes in a wide field
of split paths. "This one is rest,"

I say, "This one is sleep. Then love."
The man is silent, calm eyes.
He is the game. "Good shot," he says. There's ice
melting on the street: something glistening
into something dark.

A LANGUAGE

There's a story
of a young woman walking by mistake
out onto an unfinished bridge,
being blown off, falling,
being caught by a welder,
his arm wrenched from its socket,
the two of them making their difficult way
up into the dark, miraculous
street. She takes a pair of wire cutters
from his belt, rips part of her skirt
to make a sling. He will learn more
of her carefulness: how she shakes out
a tablecloth, folds it
into panes. Now, because they don't know
each other, there's an intricate
balance between them, as in tending a horse—
the glancing, diagonal approach
with the bridle; the cleaving
to the animal's left side, currying
and mounting. There's the woman's
sudden sympathy for the man's face, that makes her
search into it a long time—the man's eyes
elsewhere—on the stiff rays
of pine needles, at whatever has settled
in the tall grass. When he looks up
at her, it's as if there's a balcony,
a stiff wind with his hat
sailing into it, tagging away
toward a far body of hills.

I know a time when a bridge
fell, heavy with traffic in a winter
dusk—a fracture and the two sides
sheared away. Each person on the bank
with the secret thought—"I was *right*
not to believe in it."
So in the middle of the night
I rest my hand on your hip
to have it apprehend a quiet
form, a body, whole.

           for Michael Ondaatje

THE KIND OF THING THAT HAPPENS

No one else she knew gave anything
to hope, so it was up to her.
She helps things,
takes up the slack

between what should have happened
and what did. No matter there's nothing
in it for her, that she's in for as much
as if she cursed the world

up and down every day. She has
her version—all flawless
weather and rewards
for the deserving, nothing

for fools. Only now and then
she feels it, what isn't here—
hearing the noise of wind,
watching an empty box kick over

onto its side. When, climbing
barefoot up the stairs,
her heel comes down
on a cold penny.

NIGHT WORK

Night's webbed. Even when I walk
in the middle of the street,
it catches me
with sticky threads. Insomniacs
see a woman doing a *tarantella*
to shake something invisible.

At my door some mornings
there's one strand
like an oceanless
line of surf, a drowsy bridge
nothing to nowhere.

Cobwebs appear wherever our lives
don't, wherever is loneliest.
If you can gather enough
they make a good poultice
for whatever's missing.

Since spiders make webs more or less
from nothing, they never
dissolve—just reassemble
some other nowhere, somewhere
like an endless snowy field
where potters throw out their shards.

BODY

"A ghost, a real ghost/Has no need to die: what is he except/A being without access to the universe/That he has not yet managed to forget?"
— Randall Jarrell

Her small body appears again
for a moment: a little girl
in a stiff dress, crinoline.

The past has drifted away—quiet,
murmuring, backward. Her season's a sad
and sorrowful early nightfall
of muddy rivulets. Debris, barges,
stone, rock, snow, and minerals
surrounding her flat, ponderous
heart. That sends her back
through the wind's rebuffs
to a space through which light,
sounds, and air can't pass.
House that drifts
with the snow of that
left unspoken. There
is the love of her life. His eyes
the right eyes—which she sees again
in delight and detail
through sadness, distance. The lover

always imagines the loved
as alone. Alert
and spectral, walking
by a roadside. All himself.
She likes to resemble him
in walking somewhere. On a road
a burnished canal threshold to threshold.
One tight little house
with a clothesline that seems
the mooring of an ark.

LOFTY CITIES

One person lives by her eyes, another
by his nose, another accepts no pain
that's not supposed to exist.

Another keeps her most prized resolve,
"I'll stay in this narrow space,"
and so ruins her life.

Emotions are hard
to separate, except a time
when we happen to love
a whole body without
even knowing about it,
all its special lights.

People seem a loose string
of echoes starting
from silence, not even
the weight of a bone.

A car goes by, a boy
sticks out his head
wearing a paper crown.
The sky no more than a shrug
of cloud, worn out, hanging.

The best scenery is not this ridge
collared with trees
or even the unknowable
mountains and crystalline
valleys, but something
in the way of two stars
I caught sight of, falling, their two
slight sweeps down.

There are the women who wear out
the afternoons at lunch counters:
customers and waitresses
wearing one sad patience,
shreds of mother love
and slow cares. Finally
they'll leave to the streets,
though there's nowhere much
to walk to, and it would be fine
to forget all they are
and what has burned there.

Two

ELEGY FOR EDGAR ALLAN POE

From birth the mind of Edgar Allan Poe
builds itself away from the air,
thrives on quiet
and sadness, fingerless hands,
the teeth of beautiful women,
infinitesimally trembling pulses,
heads—old heads, catacombs,
the curve of a lost face turning
among stars.

The obsessed are the great specialists.
They know that love is measured
by the strength of its detachment,
the deadlock of fear and desire.

That *haunted* means simply,
this place isn't ours, it belongs
to people who've vanished, who want to share
our hearts' true loneliness.

That *dread* is to be alone
with any regularly occurring sound.

That to succeed utterly
is to place yourself at the center
of the one inevitable design
for your perfect destruction.

Angela Ball

KEATS IN ROME

Rome—latticed towers,
St. Peter mined with catacombs,
the sky lettered with birds—reduced
to hot midday light
combed through the lower blinds.

For one hour
of what's in the world—
a man pushing a boy in a wagon
whose tongue scrapes the ground,
tincture of new leaves,
combers of hyacinths,
a cricket, an ember,
a river's shift of sparks
in the wind and air.

I wrote: The animal has a purpose,
his eyes are bright with it.

To write anything, sign
a kite tail signature
made of loops and little balloons—

I tire of death's attention.
Fool, I wrote Fanny I had two
luxuries to brood over: her loveliness
and the hour of my death.

I thought
nothing else so light, so delicate!

Possession

Death—imagine trying to get something—
a pen or a shirt—you're offended your hand
won't reach. That's it—but every minute,
day, hour.

Fanny, out of politeness
toward death, stopped
calling me Love.

While we're laughing
the seed of some trouble lodges
in the wide land of events.

Infinity's gone flat.

Roses aren't mine, nor her,
though she came to stand in the garden
when I asked, to let me glimpse
her figure there.

What's me? There's more life
in any quiet corner. Moments
a memory lurches forward,
disappears, leaving a pane. Tabula rasa!
The broad dark background
when I close my eyes.

Angela Ball

CAPTAIN COOK

1. The Hero

He travels on impulse
like oceans, thinks nothing
of survival. Is one body.

Keeps a log. "Dangers
fly back and forth
over us, sometimes descend."

His job is to keep the ship
whole, keep it from scattering
the waves. To hold onto the cargo,
increase it.

2. Travel

The ship's christened *Resolution*
with the champagne of pure light.
Sky's the wide lid
of a treasure trove.

From the South Seas, Captain Cook
goes looking for the Northwest Passage,
commerce's true cross. At latitude
70° 44' a wall of pack ice
deflects him south.

South 2,000 miles—and a bird's cry,
a single dolphin all there is
to witness above water.
Too much nowhere.

Cook finds Hawaii, anchors at Kealakekua Bay.
In his dealings with Indians, Cook took direction
from them. If they were friendly,
so was he. If they wanted a god, model
for a fine feather cloak, O.K.
At Kealakekua, Lono's festival is in progress,
and Cook fits right in. The priests lead him
to an altar, feed him pieces
of sacrificial pig. For fifteen minutes
the priests perform chants and responses.

At night the ship rides at anchor.
Cook looks toward shore, sees moving torches,
their light revealing an occasional hand or arm.
Below deck native women and sailors play.
For presents, the sailors prize out nails
from the timbers, so that each act of love
loosens the ship a little.

After Cook leaves, the islanders look everywhere
for things lost from the ship, bits of iron, scraps
from the other world.

Angela Ball

The *Resolution*'s caught in storms, damaged.
Cook can drift ahead, watching for a place
to put in, or beat back to Kealakekua, be a god again
for whatever it's worth. He goes back.

The short version: Lono's welcome
is gone. Cook ends up mobbed
on the beach, kills a man with one musket shot,
tries to reload. He turns to look at the ship,
is surrounded by clubs and blades, finished off,
floating in clear, blind shallows.

His thoughts' tight rigging readjusts
to take his death
into account. "Now I'm entering
the hole, the nowhere I always suspected
everywhere inside the world."

A mountain behind him. Flowers, melon color
confused with white, petals reversed,
spilling. Stones in a gold breeze.

Waves riding over waves.

3. Funeral

Cook's effects are auctioned. The ship
has been at sea a long time, and the sailors
are short of clothes.

At first all Cook's officers can get back
of him is a piece of hindquarter.
About the other parts, reports vary:
someone saw some entrails
on an altar, thought they were an animal's,
ate them. Finally enough bones are brought forth
to compose an ocean burial.

In 1825 some British officers mark the place
with an engraved metal plate
nailed to a post. Every visitor goes down
to the water's edge for a small stone or two
or a chip of rock.

For years his death is bragged
by any islander remotely old enough
to have tossed a stone.

The day before Cook died
a chief visiting the ship asked
"Who are the warriors here?" The captain
held up his scarred right hand.

Angela Ball

DESPERATE REMEDY

Next stop, the river!
The young artist jabs
a cheap tomato
he's eating, puzzles
at the color in a globe
of vinaigrette.

What if I jumped,
and the short sky
were a lake reeling me
a whole past of blue,
blazing—so long!

Instead of the way people
seem to go down,
scraped across a file
of memories!

I'd like to look
convincingly miserable, but how much
feeling *could* I attract
as the prongs of a dead man?

I'll stay down here
at the cafe, deserted by clouds,
where a leaf's thin hand
paints itself—indelible—
to the table.

CHARM

I'm sure the red of a girl's hair
remembers its red ancestry.
That a hill keeps tabs
on its fine violets.

It's good to lean on the last,
on the next, the way July
props its feet on August
and bridges recast
their impervious shadows.

The way the wind picks up wind
as it goes, shacks up
with the crows' nests
shading high trees, and dust
hails dust as a farmer walks
trailing the cracked thews
of a harness past weeds
grown almost to full height,
whistling into air—which is what,
Shakespeare says, Antony was left
doing.

POEMS FOR ANTON CHEKHOV

Angela Ball

FIDDLE MUSIC

It's silly, knowing ourselves,
to think anyone
strong—but again
we're fooled into trembling,
pleading "—please—not me." Hit
someone else. That was the power
Yakov had over me.
He left me this fiddle.

People pay me well
to play his tune again
and again, blank old summons
of fate. Listen—

Here Yakov, the old miser,
stuffs his pipe with ashes
to smoke them again. This
is his wife, her face
pulled down into the shape
of a starved flame. Listen—
here's the river
where they picnicked
with a yellow-haired child.
Her child and his. Long gone.
The riverbank's worn down,
too near the water
to sit on anymore. And the trees—
listen—leaf on leaf
chewed by the mouths of a million
caterpillars.

Everyone listens to the tune, its fine
sadness. Everyone weeps.

Angela Ball

THE KISS

I open the wrong door
at the Lieutenant General's
party, into a completely dark room,
only a chink of light
from the door, the fragrance
of violets, the far-off sound
of a mazurka. Then there's the rustle
of a dress, a woman's voice, "At Last!"
her arms around my neck
and the sound of a kiss. The woman screams
lightly and jumps away, and I rush headlong
out of the room. Then there's the party
again, and the May evening, and me—
shy, nondescript. How can I recognize
someone I've never seen, a woman waiting to kiss
someone entirely different? I can only
compose her from my favorite parts:
the arms and shoulders of this one, this blonde hair,
high forehead, slight smile. It's impossible
even to know exactly what kiss
I stumbled into, what her lips meant.
She must have been desperate
to make him happy, but instead, me!
And how much more. If only she knew
what men say among men about their eager
lovers. If only I could have
a minute with her in the light
instead of going back
to my gray tent, pale lamp,
some cardboard sleep.

Possession

The kiss spreads itself over everything,
ordinary camp life, the regiment's
hats, legs, horses. Often I wake up
full of my secret, needing to rush somewhere
and do something right away—
leap back into the dark room,
but it's impossible, like love
from beyond death or between people
who don't exist.

Finally the regiment returns
to the General's town, and I ride
by myself up to the house—see the garden's
flowers, and the long windows—
and suddenly it's all silly, the world
nothing but jokes—and me
the most pitiful.
When I get back to camp
and find a note inviting me
to the General's party
I stifle the flare of joy
and go to bed.

Angela Ball

THE LADY WITH THE PET DOG

Once I'd seduced her, there was no hurry.
I cut a slice of watermelon, ate it deliberately.
Afterwards we walked on the esplanade,
her white dog trotting behind us.
The shore seemed dead. A single boat rocking
a sleepy light, the sea's muffled sound,
monotonous.

Things are as they are—but occasionally
some understanding opens. Back in Moscow
I saw a young man I'd always considered
an obnoxious fool
helping an old man out of a carriage
and realized this was his father,
this burden.

And something curious—my thoughts
stayed with Anna—not about her, but in her,
somehow—a stream of sad and delicious
reveries. Everything else
that was was tedious: my family,
my little son's first steps—all of it
incidental as a breeze
tapping the shutters.

Possession

I went to Anna's town
to find her. In a world that shows nothing
of its real face, how easy to decipher
the routine of a life! The premiere
of an opera, *The Geisha*—she'd have to go.
Her husband sat beside her, a hand
resting dully against her neck. I waited
while music gusted and fell silent.
Characters came and went:
a tall man in a red cape,
a woman in a costume that cut her in half—
huge front, tiny waist, rump
that seemed to drag an enormous anchor.

At intermission Anna's husband went out
and I approached, said "Good evening."
She sat staring—I stood, afraid
to sit down beside her. Together we jumped
at the blast a horn made tuning up. She rose
and hurried toward an exit. I followed, past
chests wearing badges, racks of jumbled
fur coats, the smell of stale
tobacco, a dozen bored conversations.
At the last place in the world, the entrance
to a narrow, gloomy staircase, she stopped
and we kissed, like man and wife,
like tender friends.

This is how we found ourselves in love
with no escape, the end still far
from our reach.

Angela Ball

THE DANCE PIANIST

Last night I talked to a woman—
she approached where I sat
resting at the keyboard and we talked
a long time—my eyes went, I remember,
between her blue eyes and a wonderful arrangement
of velvet roses on a shelf
behind her—until someone
drew her aside and said, in a loud
whisper, "He's the dance pianist!"
Her face flushed, turned away
and I knew our conversation
for what it was: a lie's interval.
Poor woman—she's been discovered in public
talking to an object
or the wall. So this
is my lovable body!
I'd rather be Andrei Yefimich, straitjacketed,
guarding my view of the bone-charring factory
off in the distance, than here
with my animate music, my hands
silent, swift, eloquent
plastered with invisible banknotes,
performing an act of exchange.
Naked weeping overtook me.

THE MAN IN A SHELL

One day I went walking and
boom—there was Varenka,
the young lady
I'd planned to marry,
madly pedaling a bicycle
as if she were ten years old!

When I tried to warn her brother
about such behavior
he shoved me downstairs,

tumbling out of control, dignity flying away
forever, and there was Varenka:
"Ha-ha-ha."

How be a schoolmaster anymore?
How will pupils pay attention
to a man who has tumbled downstairs?
Sonorous Greek lost in roars.

Tuck in my blankets.
Things must be kept within bounds.
Draw the bed curtains.
A man should get married.
Ha-ha-ha.

Angela Ball

THEATER

A man's sitting at the theater
with his friend—whose wife
suddenly comes in, takes a seat
two rows ahead. Nearly pitch-dark,
still, her shape's
unmistakable. How can a husband
not recognize?

For ten years, unapparently,
the man's loved her. Time's frozen
open to this page, this silence
in which a spoon's clink
could sound from another century.
Figures on stage talk, pause,
talk again.

Each time, with the stroke
of seeing her, there's the sense
of at last being awake.
Then a passel of dreams.
Prophecy of nowhere!

If love existed it would be set
somewhere by water, late fall:
a river that floods and freezes,
crazed panes of it left, translucent
in stubble fields.

That's it—water with no choice
but to reflect light, and along with it
our shapes, contained
by the air's yawn
for this dark space.

Three

A NEW EXILE TALKS OF HIS COUNTRY

We've become business-like—
less and less obvious behind
the pronoun "I"—whistling
fills in, or weariness
substitutes for love.

Facts are not the creation
of lives: white light
around stars, yellow
around the moon. Spring sun
ranges white on branches,
and so on.

No way to unend it. History's
chief element is vulgarity—
its agent, the state.
What people think will bring them goods
limits everything to appetite
and appetite's plans.

No use for memory
or the eye. Whatever objects
we find ourselves holding
so as not to lose hope
and mind—

as if to try walking
with a cane made of smoke—
for ballast,
use a feather—

resourceful as the last stages
of fire, when the soot catches.

Angela Ball

REFUGIA

The poet Elizabeth Bishop is five
when her mother is removed
to a sanatorium.
Elizabeth doesn't see her again.
"Every Monday afternoon I go past
the blacksmith's shop with the package
under my arm, hiding the address
with my arm and my other hand."

Her friend's mother goes away
and comes back, but there's still
much to hide.
"Why is your name written on your socks?"
the child asks. The wavy blue letters
should say Mother instead of the sad real name
that couldn't protect her.

A refugia is a place the ice missed
during the last great age.
The animals could go on living there
and later repopulate
the world.

In the last century
people visited asylums
the way we visit zoos.
It was not unusual
to encounter an old friend
among the raving lunatics.

A 1914 film shows Indians
rowing a beautiful boat.
An eagle man stands up in the prow
and powerfully works his wings.
The boat leaps and plunges
from one frame to the next.

Angela Ball

ABANDON

"The fossil remains of ancient and medieval populations are almost entirely of adults; children left impressions too fragile to survive, or no imprints at all." — John Boswell, *The Kindness of Strangers*

Infants dropped into the Tiber
were carefully wrapped, with weights
to sink them.

*I would not leave you
without a token.*

Theologians warned,
Those who visit prositutes
may commit incest with a child
they had abandoned.

Were there witnesses?

River,
knot of a log,
stump of a door leading
deeper,
brooch,
thorn claw,
buried wrists
of mountains.

*A lucky idea.
You'll have many toys,
many neighbors.*

Current shaking
from the sea's tugs,
shallows where horses
colossus their legs to drink.

*Go with the water, your kin.
Try your way.*

Possession

Water, soft wind,　　　　　　*I care nothing. No part*
cold voice.　　　　　　　　　*of me.*

Touch like the ground's,
a gourd rattling its seed.
Nothing can make believe　　*Let me not see.*
love's necessary to life.　　　*Let me not see.*

Angela Ball

TOWNS

"There are no sagas—only trees now, animals, engines: There's that."
— William Carlos Williams, *Notes in Diary Form*, 1927

Somewhere in midcentury
things spread out, scattered
and came close at the same time—
distances suddenly efficient,
flying by night.

What about the little towns
so full of themselves once?

The people—this is crucial—
don't think of themselves as alive
in the center of things.
Potential is out of the question,
although there is a new plant,
atomic maybe, with night clouds
of orange. When it first came
it was out of context, cowed
looking: now it's the town.

Americans are good at movie sets:
they like the raw, the provisional.
The pioneers (some of them
our father's fathers—that recent!)
lined up their best chairs in front of the house
to sit and be photographed.
Then people posed with their cars, machines
with fat curves, wheels set wide.
Didn't know yet that moving
would take power, would be the one
bright life.

I don't think it's the change itself
that's so frightening, but the vacancy
behind it. I heard of a faraway
ancient village, a conversation
between a Buddhist and a feldspar man
who said, "If we take this mineral,
it will help your village." The Buddhist
replied, "Yes. But our village
will not be here."

Angela Ball

THE FAMILY OF EYES

In the 1860's, in Paris, Haussmann's boulevards—
radiant, exciting, dangerous—
tore through medieval neighborhoods.
Mutual exposure: private and public in love
in the great city.

From the rubble of masonry
a girl picks up a chain
that must have been part of a sink plug,
knots it on her wrist.

Curtains lend modesty to the ground,
mud-spattered family portraits
face the sky, swallows
curvet the new air.

All through the old city, vestiges set free:
a fox-tail from ruined cape,
boar tusk that stabbed from a mantel,
rigmarole *mortes*. Including

the poor family that once stood staring
while Baudelaire and his love relaxed on the terrace
of a new cafe: its circus
gilt and garnet, its festoons and pedestals,
its arenas of mirrors.

The father takes in a festival
of what he'll never have—
food in plenty, rest, conversation,
love—and isn't even resentful.

Possession

Baudelaire pities them, his love wants them
shooed away. Though he hates her for it,
their attitudes amount to the same:

as long as they're in the light
the family's huge eyes
demolish all: so the very thing mesmerizing them—
the celestial happiness—
isn't there.

FLASH

I remember a mirror in the first grade
bathroom—one day I stared at it, lost,
and the thought of me
being inside *and* outside
made my fists pound the sink
till the teacher came and lifted me
back to my seat.
Seems we're doubling
for several someones. Clumsy spies,
self-portrait takers
with seconds to compose ourselves
for a quick image.
Tenuous births, wandering half here
a lawn of dry leaves
gold-specked, veil of bewilderment
half drawn.
Into valleys comes conflation
of mist—then fireflies pulse as if
trying to light all that
but lighting just themselves.

REFLEX

A man decides he'll fail
and live in ruins. He imagines
the fine figure he'll make
in people's thoughts.

But what people think
depends on chance
blazes of apples, an horizon open
to rubble of low roofs,
sand blown against the camera.

So much is opaque—rain
that looks like rain,
light that's heat
along the ribs; so much
isn't thought—what's too distant
or on top of us.

Long ago in Ohio, I
walked head down,
smiled at some thought
and looked up at a couple—
a white woman and black man
who asked "What are you
looking at?" and I still wonder.

Angela Ball

DRIVE

A young woman and man ride
a straight thin highway.
He's driving—the car's light and quick,
a shadow breeze running the blunt
brushes of vermillion clover,
swimming the small fry leaves.

    We always remember the start of things.

The hour when air is big, everything.

    Love, sweet
    heart scald.

She looks at his eyes
and quiet shoulder she could love
to ease her head against.

    We remember the start to the last, further.

She thinks of herself, surprised
how much plain loneliness
her body holds. That's O.K.,
she thinks, I'm just riding.

Passing glance of a pond
covered in lily pads—instead of blooms,
doves! Then the low spirit
of a river, brown as paint,
a wing of sand thrown over it.

Signs point down dirt side-roads:
Rabbits for Sale Cheap. Night
Crawlers. New Hay.

If they keep on going
far enough, anything
might be offered.

THE PRAYER MEETING

Mother took me: Thursday night,
the church basement, all the women
praying. They kneel on the floor—
my place. In this privacy, they cry,
crying with no tears inside it, that says
all the sad things are here
at once, and the words, *Dear Father*.
And the body is heavy and it's heavy
to be a grown woman. Not energy
and softness. Not a wonderful
many-striped dress, but this:
woe and dark ground. An odd slight thought
like a key: they wish
they had never been born.
But here I am.

NO ONE BY THAT NAME

You say into the phone,
"There's no Michelle here,"
no one that name has—

You arrive in a room
empty of why you came in—

Years loosen you back
to a child looking at gullies
of low pines, scrub brush, torch berries—
all that Dad kept right.

Dad fixed the tractor blade (you helped)
by pounding the new teeth in,
rode away, king high,
over the hill pate. Mother
rattled knives and forks in a drawer,
sat at her mirror
to put on her red mouth.

They let your fists
lock you to a zinging lamppost,
electricity haywire with the scruff
of your five years—how could they?
never mind—

you've come back
as a thought
all by itself, lonely as an eyelash
in quiet air's deliberate coolness
while a truck draws a riff of leaves
down the street—

Perfectly asleep, you wake
to an extra breath,
slightly laboring—a breath ghost,
that's all, here to remember
how rain lifts a whole night
in its travels—

how cold trees antler by evening—
trees of hard thorns,
door in the wind's face—
take it or leave it—
remembering no one.

COUNTER

Me, my retired friends: Joe, Cecil, John
wear clean coveralls
as if to play at work.
Meet at the donut place
to practice our foolishness.

We sit through morning
while the blear sun
narrows its gold. Let it go.
Chicken hearts that we are,
we know a safe place.

Winter's opening along the gulf. A year ago
my wife lost a breast, lost more.

Our first house, the birds
had singing matches in the trees,
December. Gold leaves went fluttering
in minnow schools.

Where are those days?
Movers came and crated them
year into year. Clowned on the job.

Long as we're sitting here, there's nothing
in this world to mind, cry about,
die of. Nothing, nothing serious.

CHASSÉ

She barely remembers him—had no idea
the need. How to know
Grandfather would be
her best love?

In class she imagined
any day some boy would turn,
say, "I've been watching you."
School's done. She was wrong

to think things happen gently. Look
at any family, any office—
one will be the strong horse
who kicks and shoulders her way to oats.

Windows have room for yellow flowers
like ear trumpets, leaves
blowing on end like sails.
A brown dog jaunting along.

The chassé of a sheet of newspaper
lifts her. She'd like flying like that,
loosened, blind, grazing breezes.
Knowing what to know.

ADJUSTMENTS

Lovers past love imagine air
still printed with it—
the watery name
of a vanished hotel. A phantom
beard scratching her cheek,
the feeling of lace
and silk on his hands and face—
where did they come from?

Hatred breaks as well.
Another dictator falls.
Some hands extend
toward his bullet holes—

Gently, gently.

Many circle love,
never approaching,
or work up trousseaus
against marriage.

How long can it take?
Wild light unwinds
the trees, disheveled and surprised.

AIRSHIPS

"This is me on a good day
if I ever had one"
someone says, autographing
another person's work.

All confidence is acting.
Once you've seen yourself, that's it.
There's exposure
or cover, shame on both.

A woman doesn't get
what she expects—it goes
to someone else. This has to be
a mistake. The window's empty,
everything's quiet, she's nothing.

Life becomes actual only when it's us.

A man cuts his head out of one picture,
pastes it into another, on top
of another man's body. "Here I am next to my friend
the president," he says, and sleeps happily.

The sudden world—a bird's hard see-saw tune
cut by rain, bursts of waves, the wind
frisking some newspapers,
dreams gathering all day for the night.

First a bicycle, then a motor bike,
then speedier and speedier autos—
a man's story is his transportation,
the city's broken pieces that fly apart
at his approach.

In World War I, airships floated out of Germany
to drop bombs. "I can't get over it,"
wrote D.H. Lawrence, "that the moon
is not queen of the sky . . . the Zeppelin
is in the zenith of the night, golden like the moon.
A new cosmos, a gleaming central luminary,
calm and drifting in a glow of light, like a new moon,
with its light bursting in flashes
on the earth . . . so it is the end—our world
is gone, and we are like dust in the air."

Angela Ball

OUT OF CONTEXT

A woman sits looking down
from an airplane.
The scenery dazzles: sunlight,
the dream-white prongs
of a city in fog.
A motionless harbor.

This woman's been told
"You have no sense of context."

Desert now below, the mountains' dust
downing the mountains.

A long time ago, records say,
an Indian put a torch
to the family totem pole, said "They tell me
if I want to be Christian I must give up
all our toys."

Soon any observance of native custom
was illegal.

"Really we can never relinquish anything,"
says Sigmund Freud, "we only exchange
one thing for something else."

The love of the woman's childhood,
her grandfather, gave her coins
then held them for her "so your hand
won't get sweaty." Then his funeral
where he lay as if standing
inside an unlit door.

How can anyone so loved
become a phantom, frightening
and horrible?

If this plane crashed into a city
people would be horrified
not that so much death exists—
obviously it does—but that it happens
before their eyes, and all at once.

SKY

The air is way lovelier
than it has a right to be.
Everything in a spin
of bloom, everything high
and handsome.

Exactly because it's so unlikely,
there's sadness smack in the middle
of all this possibility.
Ruin and flames.

Say you love someone
with all your heart, a man or woman
who also loves you, then doesn't.
You feel infinitely dropped.
Or worse, someone offers you
more love than you can match.

Scalp me instead, why don't you?
Stretch me on a rack.
A paper airplane comes from nowhere
to hit a spot near the heart.

I watch my love, sleeping, a body
curved away from mine, but touching mine.
I don't know what to think.
Tomorrow I'll write a note: Last night
I thought of waking you.

Nerve goes.
I'm trying to trust
my memory that at eighteen, first night
in the city, it was possible
without thinking twice
to look down from the top
of a skyscraper while the wind looped
around me.

TEXT

Chekhov said that love's "either a remnant
of something which has been immense,
or a particle of something immense
in the future." Now, no big thing.

I think it's the dark center
of a torch. A large vacuum
that produces comets.

Like Caruso's singing, it occupies
the whole body, including the feet.

It should be guarded by blue flame.

Twilight still in the air
after supper, lovers stroll along
some lanes toward the country.
All they want is one moment
to lift them out of their shoes.

Some people love alone, persisting,
as though something had killed them
and they moved on through life.

A lover is seen approaching, carrying only
his hands.

When love goes, there's just this—
nothing more there. Where did my thoughts go
before they went to him, what did I see?

Love is patience, mostly.
Long patience, if you're lucky.

A woman thinks she's a new love.
No. Under her name,
she lifts in him all the lost loves.

Love is found where the border of spring,
border of fall change places.
Shoreline where the sea
unlevels and in sunlight the moon
lofts us on the backs of waves.

WORLD-FAMOUS SEX ACTS

"Words progress into the ground" — William Carlos Williams

We're subject to tricks
of two kinds. Those done by others,
those by no one.

Wind into air, weather into wind.

Love's threads and buttons
that fall apart of themselves.

No crossing between here and nowhere.

A woman in love's lost between desires—
to lie so close her breath echoes back
scented with his skin,
to lie apart
so she can think of him.

Summer comes as it does.

Rain sure as rain,
sun sure as sun.

Possession

Know all, know nothing.

Fortune-tellers trade on the belief
the world's simply *us* writ large,
birdsong voices our pain, our joy
hot to be translated.

How to express what is always and everywhere?

Rivers proud with new mud.
Thistles and goldenrod
bronzed by wind.

Well-known caves and waterfalls.
A dim doorway with a sign promising
World-Famous Sex Acts.

The bridge walked all our lives
between longings.

TALK

A visit to a great man's house.
Absorbing conversation!
Finally you go into the bathroom.
Floor a stew of towels,
porcelain speckled
with excrescence.
More than any wisdom
the image of this bathroom
inhabits you.

Someone describes "the soul."
His talk is like a cruise
on a dead lake—if only a dust speck
would come flying
to prove the earth exists.

Mr. Jones, the oldest man,
remembers the first airplane he saw:
"It was like a fish
in the air. I got scared,
but there wasn't no place
for me to go. I just looked."

Words report a thing—we are
the report, talking ourselves through,
smoke falling upward,
held back by clouds.

EMBRACE

Maybe some of your movements
belong to you—your small
scoot and hop crossing the street.
Your habit of hugging people too high
or too low, gathering a breast
or buttock by mistake.
Your way of rubbing the toe—
you just realized—of your left
shoe on the table leg
while you eat. But the rest
are all passed on through you,
us—gestures that wait
for us to take them, like worn
stair treads or the hollow
of a soft chair. As we walk
into each other, preparing to dance
or say good-bye, there's a little jump
of hope. Then our bodies
begin to listen, to offer each other
a sort of apology for feeling,
for believing
the mortality of another,
for making brief shelter of it.

THE NOTHING ABOVE THE WATER

Separate a mother and baby—
after a time
the whimpering stops.
After that, in each of them,
there's something faraway, a stare.

A woman hears that her brother's dead.
Looks out the window: now
a cardinal's adze-shaped head
means death for her, only her.

Some evenings are two: one going up,
lightening. One falling, purpling.

Where you live,
a broken-down forest,
dark grain of water
through shambles; a laugh
that half-cries—
like the spluttering of a candle
dashed with water; a leaf
strung up on a raveled spider thread.
A lake shore, the dim below-trees,
the faint half-musical
swallowing of water.

In daylight you see the water;
in darkness you see the nothing,
a long crossing.

THE ENGLISH ARTIST'S WIFE

I go into James' workshop
break a piece of clay
from the last block he mixed
from dust and water,
shimmy it into a snake.

I should ask who wants the clay,
change this to a greenhouse—all winter,
impatiens could bloom
like no tomorrow.

He made pots—like landmarks,
like the faces of fields
so high they're only rock
and ice and wind.

All of them have one clear
hole, like a place
for dread to escape.

When he was alive, working,
he banged doomsday
into the clay,
barging out the air
so the piece wouldn't fly apart
in the kiln and break the others.

Angela Ball

I'm making October, the first full month
of his death. Almost done.
The sun, moon, earth hang in a row
making the sea proud,
inking the days with rain.

I play games at night, I imagine
the continents change hands,
the oceans fly above them for a time
before falling to rest.

Everything changes, now I'm alone,
no one to know with me.

They're replacing
the double-deck buses,
the chanting conductors.
Soon, in the Underground,
the scenery changers will remove
the wooden ticket booths.

Soon I'll be one of the some
in charge of remembering
the lengthening list
of discards.

Outrage now, but soon I'll be in space
beyond it—pretending,
out of politeness, to register
what's new.

As a man, I could keep a life—
I could be a buffoon,
fat and foolish wise, and go everywhere.
But an old lady's fastened
to the formality of dresses
that she zips in back
through a kind of yoga,
and having her hair done every Monday,
old-fashioned hair.
A beauty parlor's no place,
I can tell you, for "self-actualization."

The familiar makes sense
least of all. What am I doing
wearing an apron, stirring cinnamon
apples, when James is some ash, some dust?

Or taking a walk, feeling the crush
of gravel into soft ground,
seeing the hold of air
a whirling orange rose has reached
like the first idea for a comet?

I don't remember deciding to be married.
It was that we were in it
together, that whatever happened
to him happened to me, that we had
a double appetite
for seeing. That the best thing
apart from James was to think of him—
not about, just *of*. Now there's nowhere
to dwell, and memory
is only one, and less and less.

Exiles are lucky
to be banished beyond all
recognition, beyond springs
and stars, and know why.

I think it's true
people don't change,
only stand more revealed.
And so will I
and see it alone.

                    for Maureen Tower